SNAIL & WORM

ALL DAY

by Tina Kügler

Houghton Mifflin Harcourt

Boston   New York

*To the Los Angeles Breakfast Club,
and the wiggle–waggle*

Hello!

Hi!
Guess what?
It is the best day ever!

Really?

Yes!
I broke my toy.
I fell and bumped my shell.
And I looked and looked but
I can't find my shoes anywhere.

That sounds bad.
How is this your best day ever?

Oh, it is not
MY best day ever.

Look!
Frog learned to blow bubbles.
It is her best day ever!

And look!
Caterpillar turned over a new leaf.
It is his best day ever!

Wow!
Bird's eggs hatched.
See her new babies?
It is her best day ever!

You are right!
This is the best day ever.
But I am sorry you are
having a bad day.

My day is not so bad.
I just remembered that
I don't wear shoes.

THE SPOOKY CAVE

Wow, look at this cave!
It is so dark and spooky.

Hello in there!
Hellooooo!

Hello.

A DRAGON!
Are you going to eat me?

I am not going to
eat you.

Oh, please don't eat
me, terrible dragon!

I am trying to take
a nap.

Oh my goodness,
you are so scary!

Please be quiet so I can take a nap.

HELP!

Are you okay?

Oh, I am so glad you are here.
There is a terrible dragon in this cave.

Are you talking about this turtle?

A turtle?
We have to save him
from the dragon!

Excuse me, but—

Whew.
I have never run so
fast in my life.
I need to take a nap.

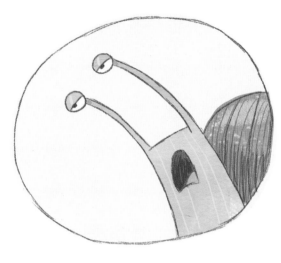

I am glad you are safe.

Please be quiet so I can take a nap.

A BEDTIME STORY

It is bedtime, but I cannot fall asleep.
I am thinking about too many things.
Will you tell me a story?

Yes, I will tell you a story.
Are you ready?

Is this a scary story?

No, this is not a scary story.

Are you in the story too?
I will be lonely if
I am in a story
all by myself.

All right.
I will be in the story too.

How can you *tell* the
story if you are also
in the story?

Maybe we can tell
the story together?

I know!
You can tell the story,
and I will add the extra parts.

That is a good idea.

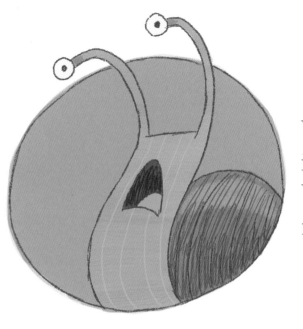

Wait, what if my story is not good?
What if you do not like my parts of the story?

I will love your story.   Really?

Yes.
You are my friend.
I like everything you do.

Oh.
You are my friend too.
And I also like
everything you do.

Boy, that was a great story
about me and you.
Good night.